WHY LOVE
Chapter 2 of
"The Life of a DL Preacher"

BY
DR. WALLACE C. COOPER JR.

Copyright © 2023

All rights reserved. No part of this publication may be reproduced, distributed, or transmitted in any form or by any means, including photocopying, recording, or other electronic or mechanical methods, without the prior written permission of the publisher, except in the case of brief quotations embodied in critical reviews and certain other noncommercial uses permitted by copyright law. For permission requests, write to the author, Dr. Wallace Cooper Jr." at the email address provided wallace_cooper2@yahoo.com.

First printing edition 2024.

Stork Publishing LLC
700 South Boulevard Dr.
Bainbridge, Ga. 39819
334-232-9281

www.lashawndashiree.info

ASK YOURSELF THESE QUESTIONS

As we embark on this journey of introspection and self-discovery, let us delve into the profound questions that lie at the heart of our human experience.

With the wisdom of age and the courage to confront societal expectations, we seek to understand the complexities of identity, acceptance, and love. From the challenges of navigating relationships to the liberating power of authenticity, each question invites us to explore the depths of our own souls and find meaning in our shared humanity. Join me as we unravel the mysteries of life, one inquiry at a time, and uncover the truths that illuminate our path to fulfillment and understanding.

- What insights can be gained from the experiences of a person reaching the age of 50?
- How does one reconcile their identity with societal expectations and personal desires?
- What role does self-acceptance play in living a fulfilled life?
- How can love transcend societal norms and expectations?
- What challenges do individuals face when navigating relationships with partners who may not be fully available?
- How does spirituality intersect with personal identity and acceptance?
- What lessons can be learned from embracing authenticity and vulnerability?
- How does one overcome the fear of judgment and live authentically?
- What strategies can be employed to break free from the constraints of societal labels and expectations?
- How does sharing personal stories and experiences contribute to collective understanding and empathy?
- And finally, how do we cultivate a sense of purpose and meaning amidst life's uncertainties?

TABLE OF CONTENT

INTRODUCTION	9-10
DON'T JUDGE ME	12-13
MY BIG DAY	14-15
CONFUSE	16-18
GUARD YOUR HEART	14-16
PHASE TWO	17-18
DON'T JUDGE ME	19-21
TOP SEXY	25
WHAT WILL $20 DO!	26-27
THE MADAM	28-29
WHAT DO MEN REALLY WANT	30-33
IF LOVING YOU IS WRONG	34-36
SIDE NOTE FOR THE WRITER "CHIEF"	37-40

GREETINGS, DEAR READER!

WELCOME

> Welcome to the world of introspection, revelation, and boundless exploration that awaits you within the pages of this book.

As you embark on this journey with me, allow yourself to be swept away by the currents of honesty, vulnerability, and unapologetic authenticity. Here, amidst the words that dance across the paper, we will delve deep into the depths of the human experience, confronting truths that may be uncomfortable yet undeniably liberating. Each turn of the page brings us closer to understanding, closer to enlightenment, and closer to embracing the fullness of our own stories. So, take a deep breath, open your heart, and let us traverse the landscapes of life together.

Each turn of the page brings us closer to understanding, closer to enlightenment, and closer to embracing the fullness of our own stories. So, take a deep breath, open your heart, and let us traverse the landscapes of life together.

May the words that follow ignite sparks of introspection, stir waves of emotion, and lead you to profound revelations about yourself and the world around you.

With warm regards,

Chief

WHY LOVE

Chapter 2 of

"The Life of a DL Preacher"

BY
DR. WALLACE C. COOPER JR.

INTRODUCTION

Does it matter who you fall in love with—male or female? If it does, why should it matter to others? My heart loves who it loves!

I wrote a book titled "The Life of A DL Preacher," exploring my experience of falling in love with a straight guy who reciprocated those feelings. The challenging aspect is that we can never openly discuss or acknowledge our relationship in public due to his straight orientation.

So, the reason for writing this second book is to understand why falling in love with someone so attractive and handsome, oh my, becomes complicated when you cannot be with them unless they decide to be open about a same-sex relationship. A while back, I posted something on my Facebook page questioning whether one should follow their heart or adhere to societal expectations. This book aims to help individuals make decisions that lead to their utmost happiness.

To explore the question of "Why Love," especially when it involves loving someone you cannot be with, is the primary focus. No, No, No, and Why, Why, Why not? The central inquiry becomes, "Is he or she in another relationship?" Being with someone they are not in love with, while thinking about the person they truly love.

Why love if you can't be with the person you love? So, why love? Love, but only when it is essential to the person you desire but cannot have. So, why love? The movie "Two Can Play That Game" only happens when you are not genuinely in love, playing a risky game that can cause harm. In some cases, there is no need to play games, especially when you genuinely love the other person. Should you come out of the closet or be free to love openly once you've fallen for someone? Or do you keep sneaking around?

A crucial question that will be asked about the first book, "The DL Preacher," is whether he or I was ever free to love the straight man. Hopefully, by the time the first book is released, I will have an answer for the world.

DON'T JUDGE ME

> **Is it okay to love from a distance, or, I would say, engage in a secret love affair?**

Is it possible to have something genuine with someone who already has a partner? Is this settling or being foolish for something you can't have exclusively for yourself? Oh my, that's the big question for today, 1/23/2022. Do fools really fall in love? Fools in love. I'm glad you asked; a fool is someone who falls in love by mistake. Does this really happen for real? Will this relationship last for days, weeks, months, or even years? Is this really possible?

"Omg, you are never unsure about love."
"Love never gives up."
"Love never hurts."
Love will support you through your scars.
When loving someone, you have to give or go without.
Love will stand still and wait for that special person. I'll wait.
Love, crying, laughter. Which one do you want?

MY BIG DAY

The heart continues to long for that which you fall in love with. But why won't it work, and the hope in the heart knows disappointment as well.

The great thing about "Why Love" is that it keeps your heart in a place that keeps pumping LMBO, why it's funny to ever think about something you can't have. It's funny to look at a BMW you can't afford, but that doesn't stop you from wanting it.

I was finally able to give my heart its copy of the book, like, after all, he does is smile all the time with such a handsome look on his face. Omg.

Why does this sexy man have to be straight? It's funny also, like he said in the first book DL Preacher, how straight guys have that good good!!! I mean, they're sexy, they're fine with such a nice body, cute butt with all the trimmings, but they're straight. Yet, you love me the way you do. Why love me like that when I can't have you!!!

> The craziest part about being in love is sometimes you're in love all by yourself - LMBO.

Why is it that most of the time, you get all these feelings, but the other person is either with you or not, so in love the way you are with them? Confusing. Shouldn't love be mutual? Leave a trick moment as just that, a trick moment. Stop allowing yourself to catch feelings for something that should only be a one-night stand. WOW! I may be confused now, but should I remain confused???

Remaining confused about love is a strange thing. Love should be given both ways, not constantly wondering if you are being loved back. Why should I ever wonder if he/she loves me? Why? Why should that ever cross my mind? Why should I use the word love if I have doubts!!! Why?

Love works both ways. I thought love is not about being used; it's about being a partner to someone you have given your heart to. No thanks to arguing. No thanks to foolishness. No thanks to the madness of being someone's dummy or fool!!!

It's crazy how straight men want to play both sides of the fence, keeping your mind all tied up on them while they live a free life and love someone else. No, no, no. We must stop giving our hearts to people who don't love us the way we love them. Why love those who don't love us back!!!! Confusion is such a powerful word once you have set your mind to fall in love with a straight guy, hoping that one day y'all will be together. Omg omg.

My heart is secretly broken, but I hide it well because I smile and still have such great friends that I talk to all the time. Some say to get over one person is to get under someone else. LMBO Omg. That's not true because true love doesn't die overnight. Sometimes people never get over true love. This is crazy. I'm writing my true feelings today about how I actually feel about the guy who inspired me to write "The Life of a DL Preacher." Omg, this is how I really feel; I must stop this and move on. How can I, once you love someone? This is crazy. We never had sex; I just gave him some of the best head in his life. LMBO SMH I hear him release inside my mouth and hold me in everything. Why can't I get over this young man? Why!!! I ask myself this question over and over again but never come up with an answer. Hell, sounds like I'm confused LMBO.

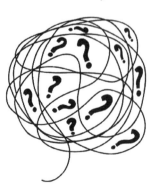

GUARD YOUR HEART

> **This part of my book is for all the bottom boys or the girls who always fall in love so fast. We must learn not to give our hearts away when we only provide good head or powerful sex to die for. Ha ha ha.**

Omg, this is crazy. I'm laughing to myself even while writing because I must like how it seems when it comes to my heart, especially when I get attached really fast.

I need to get a hold of myself. The greatest question of all times: Must people have sex without feeling? How can you do that without getting somehow attached??

Now I know bad sex omg is the worst thing that can happen, especially if that person is fine as hell. Something that you really want so bad, then you get in the bed, and his private part is small or too big and doesn't know how to use it. Omg, that's the worst thing ever that can happen to a person, and then you've been waiting to try it, and then it's the worst sex ever LMBO. Sex is bad, his head is bad, his booty is loose, OMG this is terrible!!!

Love and respect are the most important things to keep you in a balanced place in life. You only get one life or chance to live, so don't waste it on the wrong people. I love my lil Boo Boo, but he's a straight man who lives a straight life, so people on my end have decided to live a free gay life and would never try to stop him from moving forward. He gave me the best moment that had me on this path to write books about being free. I'm free and most thankful for it.

So protecting your heart doesn't mean breaking someone else's heart. Don't allow the madness of being let down to mean that you can't always have what you want, so don't do harm to someone else!!!

Hurt causes you to go or do things you wouldn't normally do, but because you're hurt, it draws you to seek revenge, but no, no, no.

Continue to follow peace with all men according to what the world says: Lust, (sex), love.

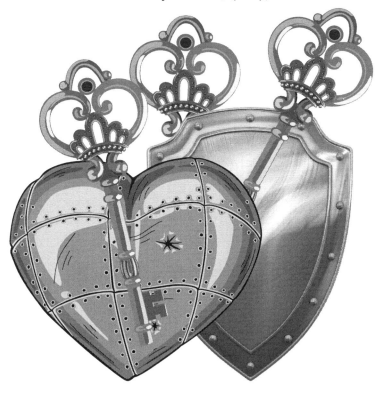

PHASE TWO

> **Question about my life with straight guys???**
> **Why do I keep allowing myself to clearly deal with straight guys that want money and pleasure but I'm looking for love.**

Love isn't in the straight guy's heart for a man; he only wants the joy of good sex and money. Once the pleasure ends, then I'm left with lust, wanting more, especially if it was the bomb!!! Omg, my love has the sweetest lips; finally, got a chance to taste them after two years. The last time we were together, it was something powerful like never before.

He did the most in a special type of something; his body began to tremble as he released inside of me. OMG, that was like never before, but the sad part is it was only for the moment (sad face).Why does this sexy man have to be straight?

Dreads, shorty, nurse, thug, and drawer are the latest of them all, but why is my heart truly with my love. Why? Being on hold means they only talk to you here and there, especially when you want more from them. Will I ever stop having or wanting to be with the straight guys instead of my own kind, meaning the gays? I just never really been attractive to the gay guys, only the straight ones, OMG ugh!!!

It hurts to never be able to have true love dealing with the straight world, but why is that they live our private, so it must remain that way!!! Can I stop this feeling I have? I want it so forced because it only leaves me wanting more.

DON'T JUDGE ME

On this Sunday morning, I sit in my home in Pelham just thinking, how can I let all this go without waiting to be entangled again by another straight guy, especially him whom I am so in love with. Most say to get over a person by getting under someone else, totally not a true statement!!!

The true statement, for most, is to guard your heart in every way you know how!!! Silent sadness hurts the most. It's to the point when you smile, but deep down, you are so sad, as I am today!!!

TOP SEXY

> **Dreads is so sexy, talking that walk, plus walking that walk for real, for real, but is an emotional wreck, to be honest. How is it that a person can make love on point, oh my God, like crazy sex, but to be honest, his mind needs so much help.**

Dreads, what's wrong? You are a great person full of love to offer, but your mind gets thrown

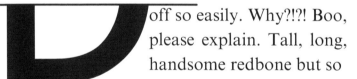

off so easily. Why?!?! Boo, please explain. Tall, long, handsome redbone but so much mix around in your head??? Why?? I know them girls love you, boo. The greatest question to myself: Why always wanting to stop but start something else with another person? Why!!! That's so crazy; this crap must stop today unless it's real, not just sex!!!"

WHAT WILL $20 DO!!!

The most powerful thing many can do is bag some great sex, even if it wasn't really planned, just for the moment. Loving the moment is better at times because they want money out, so just busting a good one really helps a lot.

I've never seen such a day where so many straight guys will give some of the best sex ever for a few dollars.

Many times in life, where you could never imagine that the greatest love can come from a straight man, is when he really wants something and has plans I don't have! Dealing with money and straight men is, to him, about how much you have to get whatever you need.

The biggest part about that is the sex that turns you on, that makes you want it more.

The fact of the matter is the love of money is the root of all evil. Oh my God, don't judge me LOL. People will lie, cheat, or steal just to get a few dollars ($20), lol, so why not get something out of the deal, a little harmless pleasure, knowing they're not going to pay back. Straight guys are so funny; they say, "I never did this before." Oh my God, I beg to differ; the way homie is making love like a pro in the sheets. Lawd have mercy—laughing out loud. My laughter is silence because, as DL Preacher says, your secret is safe with me.

The love language speaks differently behind closed doors. It speaks straight, bi, curious, or straight out gay, so Bi man, which one are you late at night or before the day in the morning? My, my, the moral of my story in the chapter is that having more with less can get you whatever you want in today's world. Most will say no it won't, but if you're not in the trap, you don't understand the trap. The trap is HELL!!!

THE MADAM

"The Madam" is a powerful word. It stands out in many cities and places around the world. Madam. I would never think of myself being that, or I'll say a mala madam, the supplier or that person people come to for money or even that deep love and passion in which they don't get at home with his girl or wife.

Again, don't judge me. Laughing out loud. I'm so serious. It's 2024, the 1st of February. I'm getting back in the groove of writing because I was just waiting for that moment where all the words began to rush to my mind. Oh my God. I'm ready to just wonder how I got to this point in my life at 50 years of age. Now, I have been through so much in life: hurt, pain, omg just trouble from one end of life to the other. Madam, do I have the "Idiot" light on my head where all the straight guys can only see it when they walk in the place? The hot light is on for real, it must be on for the straight guys to see it. My first book, the "DL Preacher," talks about the guy next door. How if you thought or even wondered who really on the "DL," you wouldn't ever know because they keep their business to themselves, the way it should be for real for real. Sex, Money, or love, which one is best? Sit back and ask yourself the question of all times. Oh my God, I know, I know they all three work perfectly together. Imagine having someone who really wanted money but it turned out to be sex, now it's a private love affair. Who would ever think a straight guy, I meant straight gay, who never thought of being with a man ends up falling deeply in love to the point he didn't want to let you go even though he can't be with you in public, but he knows you are the best thing ever to happen to him in private. That's crazy OMG for real for real.

WHAT DO MEN REALLY WANT

The greatest question that most relationships need to sit down and have an open and long talk with one another.

I mean, for real, without being upset. I talked about this in the first book because there are a lot of secrets or I'll say hidden desires most people have in their hearts or minds growing up or even being grown that they never got out of their system before they connected with their spouse or partner. So, this is something I found out being on the DL, or I'll say gay, in my 50 years. People need to really share their hearts and thoughts with their mate.

Mates???? IDK today most people are open to threesomes anyway or like both sexes on the low!!!

This topic is for my straight brothers that are playing on the low "Your secret is safe with me." But what do you really want??

As a man, been married twice, but now really living my truth, I know what I want is a darn good brother who's got his business together with some real love in his heart for me and me only!!! For real, for real. You go home to her, you sleep in the same bed, even make love to her, call her wife, bae, or even boo, your snack, all those little pretty names, but come over here and do the same exact thing. You don't make love to a trick; you hit and go—you don't passionately kiss a trick; you dap and go. You don't hold, hug, grab a trick. You never should embrace, just dap and go.

So what's over here that you're embracing, making love, kissing so deeply busting over and over again over here just to go home texting or sneakily calling, deleting messages to see what I'm doing or even riding to make sure no one else is around to protect that which is not really yours.

So what's over here that you're embracing, making love, kissing so deeply busting over and over again over here just to go home texting or sneakily calling, deleting messages to see what I'm doing or even riding to make sure no one else is around to protect that which is not really yours.

So, my straight brother, what do you really want from a gay man that you will never have in public?? It's to the point no one will even know because your "secret is safe with me," but my question is why??

Is it because of the extra movies that you got or the good sneaky link sex with no strings attached?? Which one is it, my straight brother? Please tell me or even her because Bae needs to know!!! I hear most say people like their cake and eat it too!!! Is that correct? Some say a man knows what a man really wants better than a woman does!!! Is this true, my brother, or just enjoying the best of both worlds? OMG LOL The best where you whisper in my ear "I never had anything like this before" OMG SMH Bro!!! Stop it, I say!!! You probably told my dear sister "wife's girlfriend" the same lie.

Bro, what or who do you really want? Do you prefer us both at the same time LOL? I know you wish, boo. I'm greedy, don't share, meant in the same setting LOL. I know at the end of the day the book may touch hearts or allow the relationship parties to sit back or be real with their male and ask themselves, "What do I really want?" "Question to self."

2024 means times are getting closer to the end of time; we all need to find that place of realness. No more faking in marriage or relationship or partnership, whatever ship you're in. Realness is a must today in life. I desire not to be played or lied to anymore or cheated on. If you cheated on others with me, you will cheat on me with someone else or kill that same person they left for you. We must do better in 2024. Lord, we need your help today. Life is too short for games. "Make up your mind, Bae."

IF LOVING YOU IS WRONG

This is the most powerful statement ever: "If loving you is wrong" OMG, how many times have we tried to make Mr. or Mrs. Wrong into Mr. or Mrs. Right?

OMG, it's hard but not fair at the end because most times you might get hurt, very few times you wish!!!

So why is loving Mr. or Mrs. Wrong hard to do? Why, glad you asked. Most say you must find your soulmate; we clearly know and understand they are not the right people for us, but they make you feel good and empty at the same time. Night after night, day after day, we ask ourselves, "Why are we with Mr. Wrong?" Why do they still have a connection when clearly we know they are the wrong person in the back of our heads, "Don't you?" Omg, yes, I do!!! So why continue something that you know won't last but a few hours rather than a lifetime.

Why does loving Mr. or Mrs. Wrong feel so good, but the main person at home, husband, wife, boo, or bae, that's there and doesn't make you feel the way Mr. or Mrs. Wrong does??? Why should I keep him or her, knowing it's only for one night or a few hours? Oh my, some of us love them bad boys or bad girls, omg. We love to argue or fuss, cuss, or whatever, slamming doors, hanging up the phone, then we cry after the fact, "tears of sorrow." Lord, help me to get out of this, but the moment lasts until the next time you see him or hear all in your heart, body, mind, and soul. The church calls it soul ties—it's bad to have a soul tie with Mr. or Mrs. Wrong, that time that feels so so so good, but so so wrong!!!

Being gay is funny, very funny to me, to see the straight guys who say they will never be with another guy, especially in public, but in the night he will ride him like a hawk with no problem. Have made him his private snack and all, "bad boy Omg daddy" What do you really want from Madam because loving you is so so wrong. The question of this chapter "If Loving You is Wrong" Why are you here? You're free to love all these beautiful women but choose to love me in the night. So Mr. Wrong why do you do me the way you do??

Loving on me
Hugging on me
Kissing on me
Spending late nights sending all the love messages, calling me bae and boo but you're the Bad Boy Mr. Wrong.

So we as a people often fall in love with the pleasure, good sex, and money, etc. Why is all that holding ties to my heart, body, and soul? OMG, this is so spicy thinking about loving Mr. Wrong, Bad Boy, my lips getting wet thinking about you, Bad Boy.

SIDE NOTE FOR THE WRITER "CHIEF"

Reaching the age of 50 has taught me a lot about life. I'm living my best life.

After writing the DL Preacher book, it taught me that I never needed to hide who I really was, seeing the mess many people made over these 50 years, and all I ever wanted was to be myself. I'm a free, happy, gay male who truly loves God with all my heart. A young man with little education, a former drug addict, and, among other things, at the age of 21, my life turned all around from those things. I got into the church and was called into the ministry. OMG, a big job. With many questions to God: Why would you call a gay guy like me to carry something so powerful to a world full of people always judging others? But what I love most about Christ is that He loved me when I didn't know love or even understand what love was. Thank you, my Lord.

I, the preacher, the son of the Most High, the messenger to whomever will listen, a voice crying to reach people like myself who are so scared of being themselves, wondering what the next person will say about them. But I got news, the Hell with that. Be free, my brother and sister. No one is telling anyone to go in sin, but I'd rather take my chances with God than with this flesh, which must be judged just like me.

This book is piggybacking from the DL Preacher about "The Guy Next Door." We as a people, I know my readers will understand, fell deeply in love with the wrong people that make you feel so right at that moment, which we desire to have forever. Lawd Ham Mercy, what a beautiful feeling it is at the moment. After writing the book The DL Preacher, my life became public to the world, so I had no more reason to hide who I really was. OMG, I can remember my mother asked, "Are you ready to come out of the closet?" That was the funniest thing I ever heard from her; then she said, "Baby, I got your back." God rest her soul. Her words to me were really, "I'm so proud of you." My journey is to help people like me to become free, not being ashamed of who you are any longer, but to live life to the fullest!

Opinion: your view or judgment is just that. It's not what they call you; it's what you answer to. I am free, babies, and I encourage you to do likewise. Never live life to make the next person happy while you live in regret, not living your own truth. Babies, I encourage you today. Move forward in life; never stop living your truth despite what or how the next person feels about you.

The joy I felt when my first book was released, OMG, a weight lifted off my shoulders! OMG!!! There's power in words, "good or bad," so take a moment to reflect on life to see which direction you are going. Are you living or existing??? I've learned how to live, babies. I pray you do likewise.

The greatest question of this book "Why Love Something You Can't Have." Don't answer with your lips, but answer with your heart, my love. No more hurt or pain. Free yourself from all that.

God Bless You "Chief"

Made in the USA
Columbia, SC
22 April 2024